Cuffed - A Novella

Liza Kline

Published by Sweet Anguish Publishing, 2016.

This is a work of fiction. Similarities to real people, places, or events are entirely coincidental.

CUFFED - A NOVELLA

First edition. April 16, 2016.

Copyright © 2016 Liza Kline.

ISBN: 979-8227191496

Written by Liza Kline.

Also by Liza Kline

A Joyous Romance
Betrothed to the Vampire King
Married to the Vampire King
Mated to the Vampire King
A Joyous Romance Series Bundle (Books 1-3)

Standalone
Cuffed - A Novella
The Trouble with Wedding Dates
The Fall of Diablo
Fated
The Princess & the Monk

Watch for more at sweetanguish.com/lizakline/.

Chapter 1

I put my car in park and let my head fall back against the headrest, exhaustion taking over as I finally gave my body a moment to rest. Working a double at the hospital, on three hours of sleep, the day of one of my best friend's parties was not my brightest idea. Looking at my back seat through the rear-view mirror, I could see the two boxes containing assorted bottles of wine and a bag of cocktail napkins waiting to be carried inside.

I stared at the white clapboard home my best friend Steph Williams and her brother Shane had inherited when their grandmother had passed away two years earlier. Steph had taken over the top floor while Shane had converted the basement into a space of his own. The two shared the living areas on the ground floor amicably.

There was no sign of activity coming from the house, and a quick glance at the driveway showed neither of their vehicles. Great, looked like I was lugging the party supplies in on my own. Three trips later, I slumped against the kitchen door ready to curl up and nap right there on the floor. There was no way I was going to make it until seven when the party started, let alone three in the morning when Steph's parties normally ended. It was five now; if I made it up the stairs before Steph got home, I could get in an hour nap before I had to be back down to help her with the final party preparations.

Sighing to myself I pushed off the door and made it two steps before I walked into something solid. Hands grabbed my arms to prevent me from falling on my butt. Blinking sleepily, I looked up, right into the piercing gaze of Shane. *Oh my god! I'd just walked into Shane. Don't stare; whatever you do, don't stare into his eyes.* I was losing the battle as I continued to look up at him.

Shane had been my crush all through junior high and high school. It was only when I had gone to college that I had come to the realization that my dark hair and curvy build couldn't compete with the svelte blondes Shane preferred. I came back home the summer after freshman year with fewer stars in my eyes where he was concerned and grew to accept the friendship that had developed between us. Although, in moments like this, it was hard to ignore the fact that he ticked all my boxes.

"Where are you hurrying off to?" He asked with a smirk, the dimple in his cheek making a brief appearance. God, how I adored that dimple.

"Grabbing a nap before Steph's party starts," I said, finally pulling my eyes from his and taking a step back, forcing Shane to release his grip on my arms. I rubbed my arms unconsciously where his hands had been.

"You know, after you don't answer her call, the first place my sister will look for you is the spare bedroom." Damn, he was right, and I couldn't turn my phone off or my alarm wouldn't go off. What the hell was I going to do?

I stood there for a moment, stumped.

"You can nap in my bed, if you want. It's the last place she'll look." Shane offered, leaning nonchalantly against the counter, as if he hadn't just said something outrageous, while looking better than any man had the right to. His white v-neck tee looked painted on, and his jeans clung to well muscled thighs.

Nap in Shane's bed, would I even get any sleep? Did it matter? I would be in his room, surrounded by his things. In his bed. *Earth to Alexis. You'll be alone in his bed*, I chastised myself. *It's not like he's inviting you to go to bed with him. Now **that** would be something to get excited about. Stop it! You left high school and this ridiculous crush eight years ago.*

I glanced over at Shane and saw him staring at me expectantly. Crap, he was waiting for an answer.

"Sure, that would be great," I said, trying to control my excitement.

He gestured for me to follow him with another sexy smirk, and I couldn't help but appreciate the way his ass looked in his faded jeans. I was so lost in the thought that I was following Shane to his room in the basement that I completely missed the first step.

I stumbled as I landed hard on the second step, and for a moment, I thought that I was going to pitch forward into Shane's back. I grabbed the railing at the last second, wobbled, and then stood perfectly still. Shane continued down the stairs completely unaware of our near collision. I sighed silently in relief and watched my feet as I continued down. That was close; it had been difficult enough to keep my hands to myself when we were in the kitchen. If I'd fallen on top of him, I wouldn't have been responsible for where my hands might have wandered to in all the confusion, like those delicious abs of his.

Shaking my head to clear my thoughts, I blinked at the sudden brightness as Shane turned the overhead lights on. His space was neat and organized, much like his appearance. Even when we were growing up, Shane had never been a messy teenager. The walls had been painted an off-white and featured several poster-size black and white prints of landscapes. The light gray carpet was plush and complemented the simplicity of his room.

There was an oversized sofa and recliner directly across from the stairs in a slightly darker gray than the carpet facing the right wall. Mounted to the wall was one of the largest TVs I had ever seen. Turning to my left, Shane's bed took up most of the remaining space. It was neatly made with a dark gray comforter that had two pillows encased in pale yellow cases peeking out from underneath. Apparently Shane's favorite color was gray and not blue like I had believed growing up.

"I washed the sheets yesterday," he said when he caught me eyeing his bed. "Go ahead and make yourself at home."

I yawned as I toed off my shoes by the stairs and made my way over to his bed. "Thanks for letting me borrow your bed," I said, sitting down on the edge.

"You're welcome. You know you can get under the covers," he said with a grin, this time both dimples making an appearance.

"What?" I asked, fighting back another yawn. "Oh, I know I was just waiting for you to leave. Wait, I meant I didn't want to be rude." Crap I was babbling.

Shane just laughed at me and walked back to the stairs. At the foot of the stairs, he turned back to me, "I'll wake you up in time for the party."

I waited until I could no longer hear his footsteps on the stairs before standing up and pulling back the covers. I crawled into his bed and pulled up the covers. Mmm, they smelled like him. Falling asleep surrounded by the scent of Shane was going to be difficult.

It must not have been too difficult because the next thing I knew, I was waking up in a warm cocoon of covers and masculine arms. I snuggled deeper into the pillows. Hold on, I went to sleep alone. Who was I cuddled up with?

I rolled over slowly in the arms wrapped around me to find Shane looking down at me. When the hell did Shane slip back into bed with me? And why was he cuddling me? Did I really care about when or why? Shane was in bed with me!

My frantic thoughts cut off abruptly as he slowly leaned in closer. Shane was going to kiss me. *Don't freak out!* His warm lips pressed gently against mine, and all thoughts vanished. My hands drifted around to caress his back, pulling him closer to me.

This close, I could feel his muscles ripple as he shifted against me. One hand dropped to my waist, and the other slid around to cup the back of my head, his fingers sliding through my hair. I moaned in delight as he kneaded my hip and deepened the kiss.

"Are you okay with this, Lex," he asked, pulling back slightly.

Was I okay with this? Was he kidding? I'd been waiting for this moment since eighth grade. Okay, so maybe I had only wanted to hold hands back then, but this was a thousand times better than that.

"Lex?" Oh yeah, he was waiting for an answer.

"Hey Lex, time to wake up."

What? Wake up? Why would Shane be telling me to wake up?

Shane shook my shoulder, "Come on Lex, you gotta get up."

"Just one more kiss, Shane."

"Umm, what did you say Alexis?"

"Shane?" I blinked up at him sleepily, as he leaned over me with his hand still on my shoulder. "What are you doing out of bed?"

He gave me a weird look before replying, "Come on Lex, the party already started. Steph's starting to get worried that she can't reach you."

"Why did you let me sleep so long?" I asked grumpily, hopping out of bed and heading toward the stairs, not waiting for his response. I had no desire to let him see the embarrassment that heated my cheeks.

"Don't you want that kiss, Lex?" Shane called out as I slipped my shoes on and quickly scurried up the stairs, deciding it was safer not to answer him.

Chapter 2

The party was in full swing when I reached the kitchen. I grabbed an open bottle of wine from the counter and then made my way into the living room. The overhead lights were off, but Steph had turned lamps on in each corner of the room, draping sheer scarves over them to give the room a relaxed ambiance. Not bothering with a glass, I took a swig straight from the bottle and made my way over to a group of friends sitting in the back corner laughing, probably gossiping.

My thoughts strayed to the scene in Shane's room. *What the hell had that been about? I hadn't dreamt about Shane in years, and then to have him wake me in the middle of it, could this day get any worse?* I took another long drink and tuned into the conversation flowing around me. My plan was to stay here for the night, catch up with my friends, and get drunk, not necessarily in that order. I plopped down in an empty spot on the sofa when that nasty internal voice chimed in: *you're hiding...coward!* I chose to ignore it and focused instead on my friends ribbing me about not using a glass.

"I'm helping save the environment," I declared with a stray hiccup as I glanced toward the kitchen, my eyes automatically drawn to Shane as he entered the room.

"Slow down there, Captain America," Steph said, joining our little group. "You've killed half a bottle in under five minutes."

A quick look at the bottle in my hands confirmed her words: shit; this night was not going as planned at all. I wondered briefly where my phone was. I had been planning on texting Toby, the guy I had met on an online dating site the previous week, and inviting him over, but it was probably best if he didn't meet me for the first time when I was chugging wine from a bottle.

"I'm good," I told Steph after I took another long drink and placed the now empty bottle on the table.

My drinking habit was soon forgotten as Marie asked Steph about her man of the hour. I loved my best friend but I didn't understand how she changed men like I changed my sheets, weekly. Having already heard about Brad, I leaned back and let the sounds of the party wash over me. My fingers felt slightly tingly, and I knew it was from the wine; at least my lips weren't numb like they got when I was drunk. I could handle this relaxed state of tipsiness.

A loud shout of laughter from the front of the room where the guys had congregated drew my attention. I looked over to see Shane in the middle of the group facing me. He was gesturing animatedly as he talked, probably telling another work story. Shane had graduated from high school two years before Steph and myself, and gone into the police academy three weeks after receiving his diploma. After ten years on the force, he usually had an entertaining story or two to regale friends and family with. I sometimes suspected he spiced up some of his stories to impress his buddies.

Tuning back into the conversation going on around me, I discovered that they were now gossiping about people from work. We all worked at the same hospital. Uninterested, I decide to hit up the bathroom and find something else to drink. The door was closed to the bathroom off the kitchen, so I decided to take a chance that no one had ventured upstairs yet. Luck was on my side; the bathroom at the top of the stairs was vacant.

Having completed my mission successfully, I made my way back down to the party. I grabbed another bottle of wine from the table in the kitchen and was searching for a glass, determined not to be a complete lush, when I heard more boisterous laughter coming from the living room. Curiosity taking over, I peeked in to hear Shane boasting.

"I'll show you the proper way to arrest someone. Not that shit they taught you in security guard training," he said gesturing toward a blonde guy I'd never seen before with a red party cup.

"Who wants to volunteer?" He called out to his now captive audience. And that was my cue to exit the room. But I wasn't fast enough.

"Alexis looks a little drunk and disorderly over there," Steph called out.

Shit! There was no escape now. I tipped the bottle to my lips; some things didn't call for a glass. This was one of them.

Chapter 3

How did I end up in these situations? Oh, that's right, my loud mouth, soon to be ex-best friend. I sent a glare Steph's way as I raised the bottle again; maybe if I was drunk enough, I wouldn't remember the embarrassment in the morning. Hopefully, my friends wouldn't take photos or even worse, videos of this debacle, and it could fade to a blurry memory in a few weeks.

"Put the bottle on the floor, slowly." Shane's voice interrupted my inner dialogue. I contemplated ignoring his order and giving him the finger for a split-second before noticing the intense look on his face. *Great*, he was in cop mode. Joking around would not be appreciated.

I bent over and set the bottle on the floor. *Goodbye friend,* I thought with sadness, *until we meet again.* Standing back up caused immediate dizziness. I closed my eyes in an attempt to make the room stop spinning.

"Hands in the air," Shane commanded, sounding closer than before. I opened my eyes to look at him. Damn, he looked good, still in the form-fitting white tee and faded blue jeans he had been wearing earlier.

"I said hands in the air," he repeated, staring directly at me. It was intimidating having his complete focus when he was like this. For years, I had wanted nothing more than to have him pay attention to me, and now that he was, I wished that he would find someone else. I put my hands in the air above my head, swaying slightly with the sudden movement.

"Turn around slowly and face the wall."

Seriously? I wasn't a criminal; I was an unwilling volunteer. I turned around to face the wall. It was a good thing he said slowly because right now that was the only speed I had. *Maybe* drinking bottles of wine instead of glasses was a bad idea. *Where did that last bottle go?*

"Don't make me repeat myself again," Shane's voice demanded behind me. Shit, what had he asked me? "I said step forward and place your hands on the wall. Keep them above your head." I was glad he repeated it before I had to admit that I hadn't been paying attention.

I could do that. I took two shuffling steps forward before I came in contact with the wall that separated the kitchen from the living room. It was cool to the touch, and I suddenly realized how warm the room had gotten, or maybe it was just me. I laid my cheek against the wall and sighed in contentment.

"Do you have anything on your person that can harm me?" Shane's voice was gruff in my ear, and I shook my head. "I can't hear you," he said, stepping closer.

"No."

"I'm going to pat you down now to search for any weapons or illegal substances." He said directly into my ear this time, his breath was warm against my neck.

He was close enough that I could feel the heat radiating off his body. I jumped slightly when his hands made contact with the skin at my wrists. He skimmed his hands slowly down my arms, applying a slight pressure that caused goosebumps to pop out on my skin. I sucked in my breath and held it to prevent myself from moaning out loud.

He switched to a patting motion when he got to my armpits and continued down my sides. He came to a stop when he got to my hips; his hands gripped my hips loosely.

"Spread your legs."

"Excuse me?" I said in shock.

"You heard me. Spread your legs or I'll do it for you." Shane's voice was gruff in my ear, and his fingers tightened on my hips as he spoke, like he would enjoy spreading them for me.

I took a deep breath and tried to remember that I was being pretend arrested in front of a room full of friends and strangers; not alone in my bedroom, playing sexy games with Shane, before stepping my left leg out slightly. I sucked in a nervous breath while I waited for Shane to continue his search. I wasn't disappointed when seconds later I felt him kneel behind me and place one hand on the outside of my left thigh and one on the inside. Had the wall not been supporting me, I think I would have stumbled; it had been a long time since hands besides my own had touched me there.

I leaned face first into the wall hoping that I wouldn't embarrass myself further by moaning. Shane paused when he reached my ankle, and I felt him shift slightly to the right. Then his hands were on my right ankle moving up. My thoughts took a dangerous turn; if only he was doing this when I wasn't wearing pants and maybe using his mouth instead of his hands. I could feel my cheeks getting hot as I imagined what his lips would feel like against my skin.

Shane stood up abruptly and grabbed my left wrist, bringing it down and behind my back in one smooth motion. *Damn, he's good*, I thought as I felt the cold metal encircle my wrist; a heartbeat later, the other was secured next to it. I pulled on my wrists and felt the cuffs bite into my skin. *That was going to leave a mark*.

"... understand your rights as I have explained them to you?" Shane was asking when I tuned back into his voice.

I managed to get out a quick "yes" and then waited for Shane to uncuff me so I could get back to my bottle of wine.

Shane grabbed my bicep and spun me around, "And that, my friends, is how the professionals do it." He took a bow with a grin.

I stood there staring longingly at the bottle of wine on the floor, anywhere but at the group of people laughing and teasing Shane. Why the hell wasn't he taking these damn cuffs off?

"Hey Shane," I said, trying to get his attention.

"In a minute, Lex, I'm talking here." Was he serious? He was *talking* while I stood here with my hands cuffed behind my back.

I waited until there was a pause in the conversation before trying again; "Shane," I started.

"Shh, I'm almost done." Did he seriously just shush me? Nope, that was not something that was going to happen tonight.

I wanted out of these cuffs, and I wanted out now! I bumped my shoulder roughly into Shane's bicep, causing him to take a step to the side to keep his balance.

"Get these damn cuffs off now, Shane!" I demanded in response to the glare he threw my way.

"Okay, let's go," he said with a nod to the group of guys he had been talking to.

"What do you mean, let's go?" I demanded to his back as he started to walk away.

"The key is in my bedroom," Shane said, pausing just inside the kitchen door.

"Why? Never mind, I'll wait here for you."

"They'll be off faster if you come down with me," he said. "Plus, I'm not sure I have a key here."

I took a deep breath and started to count. *One.* Just go with him. *Two.* Get out of these cuffs. *Three.* Walk home. *Four.* Call it a night. I coached myself as I finished counting.

I skirted around Shane to the basement door and realized it was closed; so much for my grand exit.

Chapter 4

I somehow managed to make it down the stairs without falling on my face after Shane opened the basement door for me. There had been a few close calls, but now I stood safely in the middle of Shane's room waiting for him to find the key to the handcuffs. My annoyance at the situation was definitely being magnified by the wine I had consumed.

"Why don't you have a seat on the bed," Shane called from the corner of his lamp lit room. *Did this family not believe in overhead lighting?* I thought snarkily.

"Maybe if you turned on more lights, you'd be able to find the key faster," I muttered half under my breath as I made my way to his bed, the rumpled covers from my earlier nap beckoning me.

I stood at the edge of the bed wondering how I was going to sit down in a dignified manner. I wasn't exactly graceful on a good day, so being inebriated, with my hands secured behind my back, was going to turn this simple task into a challenging feat. I could just flop down on my stomach, but then I'd have to turn my head to one side so I could breathe. Laying on my back with my hands digging into my back didn't seem like a good option either. Sitting on the edge of the bed held the most appeal, but there was a good chance that I wouldn't be able to keep myself balanced. Landing either on my side on the bed or on the floor in an undignified heap seemed to be a likely outcome.

Option three seemed to be the most comfortable course of action, so with a glance over my shoulder to make sure Shane was still busy searching and not watching what was sure to be a moment I'd prefer never to remember, I turned and slowly lowered myself to the bed. *Think of it as a squat*, I coached myself, hoping that I would soon be released. I felt the mattress squish against the back of my thighs and I sighed in relief; I'd done it. Grabbing fistfuls of covers as best I could, I carefully scooted myself further back onto the bed until the backs of my legs rested against the side of the mattress.

Satisfied that I was no longer in danger of landing on the floor, I glanced at the corner to see if Shane had succeeded in finding the key, but he wasn't there. A quick scan revealed he wasn't in the other corner of the room either; I was just about to call out when I heard an amused chuckle directly in front of me.

"You should see your face right now," Shane said, stepping away from what I had previously thought was a wall of mirrors but was, in fact, mirrored doors to a walk-in closet. Dangling between his fingers was what I assumed was the key to my freedom.

I chose to ignore his comment and waited impatiently for him to approach the bed. Sitting like this was starting to make my shoulders ache. Instead of focusing on my discomfort, I chose to focus on the way the shadows played on Shane's skin, as he watched me intently from his place in front of the mirror.

If I looked hard enough, I could just make out my reflection. Seeing myself sitting on Shane's bed with my hands cuffed behind me, waiting for him, started a delicious fantasy in which he hadn't cuffed me in front of a room full of people. Instead, upon waking me earlier in the evening, Shane had continued where my dream left off...

"One more kiss?" Shane asked with a playful grin, and I nodded.

I could feel my heart start to beat faster as he put a hand on either side of my head and lowered his face to mine. I could feel his warm breath feather across my face as he exhaled slowly before gently touching his lips to mine. A low moan built in the back of my throat as he deepened the kiss but was cut short when he pulled back slightly and looked at me through hooded eyes.

"Why did you stop?" I complained.

"You only asked for one kiss, Lex." That damn dimple appeared again as he continued to watch me.

"You don't have to stop at one," I said after a moment's hesitation.

"I think you have to earn more kisses if you want them."

"How?" I was intrigued by what he might want in return.

I watched the muscles in Shane's chest bunch and stretch as he leaned over me to grab something from the drawer in the nightstand next to the bed. The silver handcuffs that appeared in my vision were definitely not what I had been expecting him to get out of the drawer.

"You want to cuff me?" I asked slightly confused. The grin on his face answered my question.

I paused my wine-influenced fantasy to wonder how many other women he had played this game with before, and was suddenly no longer enthralled with the idea of seeing what would happen next.

"Are you okay?" Shane's voice snapped me firmly back into reality.

"Yup, just great," I said wondering how long I'd been lost in fantasyland.

"Ready to be freed?"

"I've been ready the moment Steph volunteered me." I said eagerly anticipating the moment I would have my hands in front of me again, where they belonged.

The bed dipped as Shane sat down next to me, and I couldn't stop myself from rolling into him. "Hi there," he said, looking down at me with a grin. "Can I help you?"

I tried unsuccessfully to push myself away from Shane so I could answer without talking into his arm. After letting me struggle through several failed attempts, Shane placed an arm around my shoulders and helped me sit back up.

"Kind of you to let me struggle first."

"Kind is my middle name."

"Liar, it's Malcolm. Or are you forgetting I've known you since I was eight? I've heard your mother yell, Shane Malcolm Williams, more times than I can count."

"I forgot you were around for that," he said, playing with the key.

"So, are you going to free me or not?" I asked, staring longingly at the metal key in his hand.

"Sure," Shane said before lying on his side on the bed behind me. I felt his warm hand on my left wrist and then heard a soft click. My wrists fell limply at my sides, and I let out a soft moan as the tension in my muscles started to relax.

"Rolling your shoulders will help." He said still on the bed behind me.

I nodded my head and slowly started to roll my shoulders. There was a rustling noise from behind me, and I looked over my shoulder to see that Shane had flipped onto his back, the cuffs and key lying next to him forgotten as he stared up at the ceiling. Catching my eye, he patted the bed next to him in a silent invitation.

As I settled in next to him, I wondered drowsily if he had ever had a woman my size in his bed before. Highly unlikely, I thought with a scoff. I'd seen most of Shane's dates, and they tended to be slender blondes; my curves would never have fit into their "oversized" sweats, let alone their skinny jeans. The image of me trying to get into a pair of skin tight jeans made me giggle, causing Shane to prop himself up on one arm and look down at me.

"What's so funny?" He asked with a look on his face that caused my breath to catch in my throat.

There was no way I was going to admit I had been thinking about the other women that had graced his bed, so I just stared up at him, studying his face. Wait a second, why was Shane giving me his bedroom eyes? I'd seen that look on his face enough times over the years to know what it meant. Hell, I'd wished for that look for years before I realized how futile it was. I was suddenly acutely aware of how close we were, alone in his darkened bedroom... in his bed.

I sucked my lip in between my teeth, a nervous habit I swore I'd break one day because it wreaked havoc on my desire to have smooth, unchapped lips. Shane must have taken it as an invitation because his head slowly lowered toward mine. I could hear my heart beating in my ears as I watched his descent, eyes locked with his. Only when I felt the first brush of his lips against mine did I close my eyes. I wondered briefly if he'd closed his as well, but all thought ceased to exist when I felt his hand on my hip; even through the fabric of my sweater, my skin tingled from his touch.

I could feel the warmth radiating off his body as he hovered over me, his fingers kneading my hip as he deepened the kiss. He nipped my lip with his teeth, and I couldn't contain the moan that slipped from me. This was even better than I'd imagined it would be. Shane's hand slipped under the hem of my sweater, and the direct contact of skin on skin was even more intense than I had anticipated.

I shifted to give Shane better access, as his hand slid up my back toward the clasp of my bra when there was a sharp pain in my hip. I pulled away from Shane.

"What's wrong?" He asked, concerned, frown lines appearing on his forehead. I was torn between wanting to make the pain stop and smoothing the lines from his face. Pain won, and I reached under my hip. My fingers closed around cold metal, and I realized it was the discarded cuffs. I held them out to Shane and then winced again when I felt something else poking my side. I ran my hand under my side again and produced the key.

"Oh." Relief was evident on his handsome face as he took both items from me. "I'll put these away for the night."

I watched him cross the room and drop them into a duffle bag by the stairs. As he turned back toward me, I heard Steph call out. "Shane, is that you down there?" Shit, I could not let my best friend catch me in her brother's bed.

"Yea, what's up Steph?" He yelled back at her.

"I need some help with the keg."

"I'll be right there." He called out as he walked back over to me. Shane crawled on top of me, and our lips met in a fierce battle. His making the first move had unleashed an intense desire I hadn't realized was just waiting to be ignited. Way too soon, he pulled back and whispered, "Don't go anywhere."

I watched him cross the room and disappear up the stairs before snuggling into the sheets wondering how long he'd be.

Chapter 5

I woke up disoriented and groggy. My head ached, my teeth felt furry, and I was pretty sure a desert had taken up residence in my mouth overnight. No more wine, ever. Who was I kidding? I'd be cracking a bottle open Saturday night with Steph at our weekly get together to discuss why we were failing at life. The previous evening flashed back to me with crystal clarity as I sat up, looking around Shane's room.

Ugh! What had I been thinking, or rather why hadn't I been thinking? This was definitely not something I could undo now that it was done. Wait, where was Shane?

I leaned back against the headboard when I realized he wasn't in the room with me. Had Shane come back from helping Steph and curled up next to me when he had found me passed out or had he walked away in disgust, leaving me to spend the night alone in his bed?

I forced myself to get out of bed before I spent the day there contemplating whether or not Shane had slept with me. I took one last look around the room before tiptoeing up the stairs, hoping Steph was still asleep.

"Good morning sunshine," Steph chirped from her seat at the kitchen table, looking way too chipper for the morning after a party.

"Were you sitting there waiting for me?" I asked, taking the seat across from her.

"Not you per se," she said with a grin running her fingers through her dark brown hair that reminded me of her brother's. "I was waiting to see who emerged from Shane's cave this morning since he disappeared before the keg was tapped."

"So, you didn't think it was me?" I asked hopefully.

"Nope. I thought you were mad at me and left as soon as Shane had taken the cuffs off." I sighed in relief; if that's what Steph thought, then that's what our friends thought, and I wouldn't have to endure their endless teasing and questioning. It wasn't like my crush on Shane growing up had been a secret.

"You don't look like you spent the night with my brother, though. Is this an elaborate joke?" She asked, giving me a curious look.

"Not a joke. I wasn't sure if he had even spent the night with me since I woke up alone." I said feeling slightly embarrassed by my admission.

"Shane works out with the guys from the station every Saturday morning," Steph said, taking a sip of her coffee. "Don't worry Lexy, he didn't run out on you."

"Don't you think it's weird that your best friend spent the night with your brother?" I asked, stunned by her acceptance of the situation.

"Well, it's not like you haven't been in love with him since junior high," she said grinning at me. "I've been preparing for this moment for years. I'm just shocked it hasn't happened sooner. Although, judging by your lack of rumpledness you two didn't do anything fun last night."

"You called him up right after he uncuffed me and I passed out while waiting for him to return. I'm blaming the two bottles of wine I chugged last night combined with the lack of sleep from working a double yesterday." I told her, some things were best left unsaid.

I froze when I heard the sound of the kitchen door opening. I wasn't sure if I was ready to face Shane yet. I should have just made an excuse and gone home instead of staying to talk with Steph. My heart started to race, and my palms were suddenly damp; I was so not ready to do the morning after with an audience.

Shane walked through the door laughing, his green eyes sparkling with amusement. My nervousness started slipping away as his eyes caught mine. He smiled, but before I could return it, a short blonde wearing cut off sweats and a sports bra walked in behind him.

Working out with the guys, my ass. Before anyone could say a word, I was out of my chair. I grabbed my purse from the counter and stomped out the kitchen door, looking straight ahead, refusing to look at Shane or his "workout buddy."

It wasn't until I reached my car that I realized my keys were still in the house. There was no way in hell I was going back for them. My house was only a few blocks over; I'd walk and text Steph to bring my keys over later.

Chapter 6

I was running late. There was nothing more I hated than being late, especially for a first date. It was rude, and I was worried that Toby would think I was standing him up and leave before I got there. I was hoping that he would be understanding when I explained my day to him; it had been nothing short of hectic.

Brushing my teeth and taking a shower had greatly improved my mood Saturday afternoon, and after getting some food in my system, I had sent a quick text to Toby, the guy I'd been flirting with through text message over the last two weeks, asking him if he wanted to meet. I'd met Toby through the dating app I used when I got tired of being alone and worked up the courage to meet someone.

Toby had immediately responded with an enthusiastic yes; well, at least I took the exclamation point after the yes for enthusiasm. Sometimes it was hard to tell with a text message. After a few texts back and forth, we settled on dinner Thursday at a restaurant in town. The week had passed quickly, and now it was twenty minutes until we were supposed to meet, and I was still in my scrubs.

Get it together Alexis! I coached myself as I made my way to my bedroom. *You have exactly eight minutes to get out of these dirty scrubs, wash off the smell of vomit, change into something semi-flattering and get in your car.*

Thankfully, Steph had dropped my car off Saturday night. She had wanted to talk more about what had happened, but I was still hurt and embarrassed by the situation. Now, I was mostly just embarrassed. *Yup, embarrassed,* I told myself stepping into the shower.

I had completely overreacted to seeing Shane walk into the kitchen with a scantily clad blonde woman, the morning after we had spent the night together. Nothing more than a heavy make-out session had happened thanks to Steph and the two bottles of wine I had consumed, but it still stung a bit that he hadn't even waited until I was gone before bringing another woman home with him. What would he have done if I had still been in his bed when he got back?

No time to think about that Alexis, I reminded myself as I turned off the shower. What the hell was I going to wear? A quick glance at my legs determined I was good to wear a skirt, which made my life easier. I grabbed a yellow, off-the-shoulder dress from the closet that got me compliments every time I wore it.

Slipping on a pair of black heels, I hurried back down the stairs, grabbed my purse from the stand by the front door, and was in my car with a minute to spare. As I backed out of my driveway, my phone rang; the number that flashed across the screen on my dashboard was the same unfamiliar number that had been calling me all week. They never left a message, and I refused to answer a number I didn't know. *Eventually, they'd get the hint,* I thought as I let the call go to voicemail.

A knock on my window caused me to jump and jam my foot on the brakes. I'd been so focused on watching for an opening in traffic that I hadn't seen anyone approach my car. A bare chested Shane was standing next to my car; I assumed he was wearing running shorts because there was a thin sheen of perspiration covering the parts of him that I could see. I had been right; he would have looked even better with his shirt off Friday night, I thought as I stared at his sculpted muscles.

Stop it Alexis! Right this second. You are on your way to meet a perfectly nice man, who won't trade you in for a blonde in the morning... you hope.

"You look good, Lex," Shane said when I rolled the window down, cringing at the mannish nickname he had given me when we were children and refused to stop using.

"Thanks, I really need to get going. I'm running late." I said as Shane rested his arms on my door.

"Don't you have a few minutes for me? I really need to talk to you about what happened last weekend." He was looking at me intensely, like this conversation actually meant something to him.

"Look Shane, there's nothing to apologize for and nothing more to say. I'm late, and I don't want my date to think I'm standing him up." I hit the button to roll my window up. Shane stepped back when I took my foot off the brake and started to back into the street. I was proud of myself for being able to talk to Shane like an adult. If he could act like nothing had happened between us then so could I.

A glance at the clock told me I had seven minutes to make it to the restaurant. Why was it that when Shane was involved, my nights never went according to plan? I sent a quick text to Toby telling him I had got stuck behind a slow car and would meet him at the restaurant shortly.

Okay Alexis, get yourself together. Don't think about Shane, focus on the great night you're going to have. Ha! You're a comedian self. How am I going to be able to concentrate on anything after seeing Shane shirtless?

Chapter 7

Toby was waiting for me by the doors to the restaurant when I arrived three minutes after seven. He was about twenty pounds heavier than the photos he had on his profile, but still attractive. He was six foot two, I knew thanks to his profile, with short dirty blonde hair, light blue eyes and a faint five o'clock shadow. The green button down and tan slacks he was wearing fit him well and were flattering. On any other night, I would have been nervous meeting him, but after my encounter with Shane, I was just happy I had something to do other than replay our conversation repeatedly in my head, looking for some hidden meaning that wasn't there.

Toby recognized me as I approached and met me halfway with a hug that was just a tad too close for someone I had just met. He smelled faintly of sandalwood, which was a pleasant surprise.

"Shall we," he asked, placing an arm around my waist, and I resisted the urge to pull away. I was slightly uncomfortable with his touchy nature.

Once inside the restaurant, Toby thankfully let his arm drop, most likely because we had to walk single file behind the hostess to reach our table. He pulled my chair out for me before sitting down himself; was he for real? Did he actually act like this or was he just trying too hard to make a good impression? I'd never seen anyone do that before; movies didn't count. I found it slightly awkward.

Toby made small talk about his day while we waited for our server to appear. Luckily, he seemed content to chatter away without much input from me. My thoughts were still stuck on Shane and why he wanted to talk about Friday night.

Shane? Was I hallucinating? It was as if thinking about him had drawn him to where I was. He was taking a seat two tables over and slightly behind ours with the blonde from Saturday morning. I pinched myself and looked back up; nope, Shane was definitely here, staring at me intently. Why did he have to pick the same restaurant I was at? It wasn't that small of a town.

Just then, our server arrived, cutting off Shane from my line of sight. We both ordered the chef's chicken special, and I ordered a glass of wine. I would definitely need some liquid encouragement to get through this night; I just wouldn't drink the entire bottle.

I focused on Toby while we waited for our meals, refusing to acknowledge Shane's presence. Toby was a decent guy, he just wasn't Shane. I wanted to bang my head against the table. It just wasn't fair. This could have been a decent night if Shane hadn't shown up at my house and then again here at the restaurant.

I picked at my meal when it arrived. I'd lost my appetite the moment I'd seen Shane and the blonde. I could feel him watching me as I sat there trying to ignore him. I gave up trying to eat and put my fork down. At least I'd have lunch tomorrow that I didn't have to make.

"Is everything okay," Toby asked, looking concerned.

"I'm fine. Just not as hungry as I thought," I said, forcing a smile. It wasn't his fault that Shane had ruined my night.

"Would you care to dance?" Toby asked. I was caught between not wanting Toby to touch me again and wanting Shane to see me in the arms of another man. My desire to show Shane that I could care less about him won out.

I nodded and stood up from the table. Toby put his hand on the center of my back and guided me to the small dance floor in the corner. There was an elderly couple in the middle of the floor, swaying back and forth to the classical music the pianist was playing. Toby took my hand and pulled me close, invading my personal bubble, again, leaving barely an inch of space between us.

"Umm, Toby," I started, searching for a way to tell him I needed more space without hurting his feelings as we started a slow two-step.

"Excuse me," a voice I knew all too well interrupted. Toby paused our movement to acknowledge Shane.

"Can I help you," Toby asked, his voice deepening and his hold on me tightening.

"I'd like to cut in and dance with the lady if she's okay with that," Shane said, ignoring Toby, watching my face as his words registered. *Was he serious?* He showed up with his own date and now wanted to cut in while I was dancing with mine. This was outrageous! I could feel my cheeks heating in anger.

I felt Toby's grip on me loosen as he turned to Shane, "The lady is here with me. I suggest you go find your own woman if you want to dance."

Toby was now squared up to Shane; this would not end well if I didn't do something. Shane wouldn't back down, and it didn't look like Toby would either. Shane had a good two inches on Toby, and even though Toby outweighed him by at least fifty pounds, Shane was a wall of muscle. I had to stop this before it went any farther.

I put my hand on Toby's chest, "It's okay. He's my best friend's brother. He probably just wants to check up on me. He's a cop, you know." The word cop seemed to lower Toby's ire considerably, and he took a step back.

"Fine." Toby stalked back to the table, not at all pleased with the turn of events. *Well, neither am I, buddy*, I thought to myself crossly. I'd rather still be crowded against Toby than stepping into Shane's open arms, and to think I had been worried about coming across as rude.

"What do you want?" I hissed at Shane as soon as Toby was out of earshot, "And where the hell did you find dress clothes so fast?" I asked, annoyed that he'd shown up at the restaurant only minutes after my arrival looking like he had stepped out of a magazine ad.

"I told you we needed to talk, but you didn't want to listen." He said looking annoyed; with what, I had no idea. "And I keep a suit in my truck for work."

"I told you at my house that there wasn't anything left to say. Were you trying to ruin my night by making me late and then showing up at the same restaurant with the woman from Saturday morning? Did you really need to rub her in my face again?" I was furious that he thought his interference in my life was acceptable behavior.

"I've been trying to call you all week, but you won't answer my calls."

"What are you talking about?" Then it dawned on me, the calls I'd been getting from the unknown number. "Wait, that was you? Why didn't you leave a message? I didn't know the number, so I didn't answer."

"This isn't something I wanted to discuss through voicemail, and I knew you wouldn't return my call if I did leave a message."

"That should have given you a hint. I don't want to talk to you," I said hotly.

"Lex, we need to discuss what happened between us," he said softly.

Looking into Shane's green eyes, I was suddenly very aware of the way his hand cupped my hip and the fact that he had laced our fingers together as he twirled us expertly around the small floor. It was strange to actually be dancing instead of the usual side to side step, the few men I had danced with over the years had done. I could only smell a faint hint of Shane's cologne; apparently he didn't keep that in his truck too. That scent had followed me home Saturday, and I had spent the rest of the weekend torn between wanting it gone and never wanting it to leave.

The reminder of the weekend brought me back to the present. Shane had no right to ruin my evening. Toby was a nice man and didn't deserve to be pushed out of his own date by a man who didn't even want me. The song ended, and I pulled out of Shane's grasp and walked off the dance floor. Toby wasn't sitting at our table, but the blonde was still sitting at Shane's.

Maybe he'd gone to the bathroom, but I had a sinking feeling that he'd left while I was dancing with Shane. My suspicion was confirmed when there was a note sitting on top of my boxed up leftovers. Toby was a good man; he didn't deserve to be treated the way Shane had acted on the dance floor.

Dinner's been taken care of. I won't be made to feel like second best. Please erase my number from your phone.
Toby

I could feel my anger growing again. Mr. Handsy was lucky I had stepped in when I had, but was he grateful? No. He thought I was choosing Shane over him, and instead of talking to me, he had slunk away like a spoiled child. Screw it! I was done with this crap.

I could feel Shane standing behind me, and I wanted nothing more than to scream at him for wrecking everything. Did he not realize it took two months of screening losers and creeps before I'd met Toby? And then not even five minutes into our first date he shows up and destroys everything. Instead, I picked up my to-go box and walked out of the restaurant, refusing to give Shane the satisfaction of looking back.

Chapter 8

Steph had assured me that Shane was working. It was the only reason I was willing to go over to their house tonight. I had no desire to see Shane anytime in the near future after Thursday night's debacle. He had called several times Thursday night, three times on Friday, but today he had been surprisingly silent. Not a single call. His sudden silence made me slightly nervous that he'd be waiting for me, but I was mostly convinced that he had taken the hint and given up.

I pulled into the Williams' driveway searching for signs of Shane or his truck. I was being paranoid, but the last time I thought he wasn't home, I had literally run into him within seconds of walking through the door. I peeked in the garage just to be safe before walking into the house.

"I'm here, Steph," I called out, setting my things on the kitchen counter.

"In the living room," she responded. "I have wine." There was a god.

"Where's my glass?" I asked, walking into the living room.

"Here you go," she said, holding out a glass to me. "Have a seat."

I curled up on the loveseat across from her taking a sip from the glass she had just handed me. "This is good." I said with a sigh. "How was your week?"

"Not as interesting as yours." She replied with a knowing grin.

"Oh god, can we not discuss my week?" I pleaded knowing that's all my best friend wanted to do.

"My wine, my rules," she said as I groaned.

"Fine, but I'm going to need more wine if that's the case." I said, downing my glass in a gulp and holding it out for a refill.

"**S**o you've been avoiding his calls?" Steph asked when I finished giving her the details of my Thursday evening.

"Of course," I exclaimed. "What could he possibly have to say to me that would make any of this any better? I just want to forget the last week ever happened."

"So, what are you going to do?" Steph asked, holding out the bottle of wine to me. "It's not like you can avoid my brother forever."

"Wanna bet?" I asked as I topped off my glass, emptying the bottle. "Besides, I'm sure his blonde friend will keep him busy for awhile, and when he gets tired of her, he'll find another one and then another one after that. It will be easy to avoid him."

"Is that what you think?" Shane asked from behind me, causing me to jump and nearly spill my glass of wine.

"What are you doing here?" I demanded throwing back the wine remaining in my glass. Liquid courage was definitely needed for this situation.

"I live here."

It dawned on me then that Steph had set me up. "Really Steph? You tricked me?"

"I didn't plan this, I swear," she protested standing up. "Shane texted and asked what I was up to, and I told him you were here."

"How could you?" I stood up too, feeling betrayed.

"Don't blame Steph," Shane said, and I whirled around to face him. The blonde was standing next to him; at least she was fully clothed this time.

"What's she doing here? Haven't you had enough of rubbing it in my face that you picked her over me? Fuck you Shane! Just leave me alone."

I stomped out of the living room and into the kitchen, grabbing my purse off the counter on my way out the door. I slammed the door on my way out. I had an eerie sense of déjà vu as I started walking back to my house. This was starting to become a habit I needed to break, quickly. I couldn't believe Shane. Why did he feel the need to continually make my life miserable? What had I ever done to him? I wasn't the one who had initiated things last Friday night. That had all been Shane. So why was he torturing me?

"Alexis Marie Thomas! Stop right there!" Shane called after me.

Chapter 9

I froze the moment I heard my name come from Shane's lips. He actually knew my full name? Wait, that didn't matter; Shane was still an asshole. *Keep walking; don't engage him. If you respond, you're letting him win*, I told myself as I continued down the sidewalk.

"Don't walk away from me," Shane called after me. I kept walking.

"Where are you going, Shane?" I heard a feminine voice I didn't recognize yell in annoyance.

"I'm doing something I should have done a long time ago."

"But, what about.."

Shane cut her off, "I don't care, Rachel. Tell him whatever you want to, but I won't be there."

So the blonde had a name. I briefly wondered who 'he' was but it wasn't worth my time. I noticed curtains twitching in some of the houses lining the street. Great, all their yelling was attracting the attention of the neighbors. Just what I didn't need. I walked a little faster. I really should have driven home. I'd have been there by now, but with my luck Shane would have pulled me over for driving impaired.

I saw my house as I rounded the corner, finally. It had been silent for about a block, so I gave into temptation and glanced quickly over my shoulder. Shane was about five hundred feet behind me, walking like he didn't have a care in the world. His calm demeanor just served to elevate my anger. How dare he? He had no right to look so care free when he kept disrupting my life. I wasn't some toy he could play with whenever he felt like it.

I grabbed my keys from my purse as I approached my front door. I needed to get inside before Shane could stop me. I heard the scrape of his shoes on the walkway behind me as I attempted to slide the key into the lock. It wasn't going in the lock; did I have the wrong key? I glanced down and realized my hand was shaking. Damn it, I was not this person.

"Let me help you, Lex," Shane said softly from behind me. I could feel him standing slightly behind me. I knew that I couldn't win in a fight against him for the key; my shoulders slumped in defeat as I gave in. I hadn't realized how tense I was until that moment. I dropped my keys into his outstretched hand without looking at him.

Shane reached around me and unlocked the door before handing them back. I opened the door, dropped my things in their usual place on the table by the door, and headed straight to the living room. Once I was seated on the sofa, I looked up at Shane. He was standing just inside the living room watching me.

"What do you want Shane," I asked tiredly.

"Who do you think Rachel is?" He countered. I frowned at him; did he really follow me here to play childish games? I took a deep breath to give myself a moment to compose myself.

"Did you really follow me home to discuss your latest girlfriend?" Then it dawned on me: he was worried I would tell her about Friday night. "I won't say anything to her about what happened."

Shane let out a sharp laugh that startled me. "She already knows. I told her Saturday morning." I sat there confused. It must have showed on my face because he continued. "Rachel is my partner. She left her glasses in my car Friday and was picking them up."

"You were laughing..." I started, letting the rest of the sentence go unfinished when I realized how petty and jealous I sounded.

"I had just told her about how I'd finally gotten you in my bed when Steph interrupted, and then when I got back, you had fallen asleep." Shane said with a sheepish grin as he walked farther into the room, now standing only a few feet away from me.

What did he mean by finally? I'd known Shane for almost twenty years, and not once had he shown an iota of interest in me. I would have known, I had been infatuated with him growing up. He had always treated me like he had treated Steph, casual indifference.

"Why are you messing with me Shane?" I asked, perplexed by his sudden interest.

"I'm not, Lex," Shane said, moving closer still. "I've wanted to date you for years, but you always treated me like Steph's older brother. I took a chance last Friday night and hoped it would pay off. I didn't expect you to freak out Saturday morning when you saw Rachel. I thought we'd have time to talk when I got back from training. Then you wouldn't return my calls."

He knelt down in front of me. "I was hoping you wouldn't say no to Steph when she invited you to come over tonight. I texted her every twenty minutes asking if you had gotten there yet. I needed to see you after Thursday night."

"Why?" He looked down for so long I thought he wasn't going to answer.

"I can't stand the thought of you dating another man. Spending time with him, cuddling with him, sharing your bed with him. When those are all the things I want to be doing with you. It's all I can think about." Shane admitted looking up at me through his thick, dark lashes.

"You're crazy." It was the only thing I could think to say.

"About you," he said with a self-deprecating chuckle.

"I'm not sure what to say right now." I told Shane, staring over his shoulder at the pictures hanging on my wall. It was hard to think with him this close to me.

"Just say you'll give me a chance." He said as he got up and sat next to me on the sofa, invading my personal space as his thigh pressed against mine. "That's all I want, Lex, a chance to be with you." Shane's arm wrapped around my shoulders, pulling me tight against him.

I briefly wondered if I was having another wine-fueled dream and would wake up alone in my bed. But, if that were the case, there would be far fewer clothes involved right now. So this was actually happening, holy hell. What was I going to do? The teenage girl inside of me was jumping up and down for joy, but what about the adult me? What did I want?

Who was I kidding? I was ready to start jumping up and down too; Shane wanted to date me! I must have been taking too long to respond because I felt Shane's fingertips on my chin, gently turning my head to face him.

"So, what do you say, Lex, will you give me a chance?" He was giving me those damn bedroom eyes again.

What did I have to lose? It couldn't be worse than the past week. If I said yes, I wouldn't have to live with the regret of never having had a chance with Shane. He was offering me one on a silver platter. Besides, those green eyes of his were hard to resist.

"Yes," I managed to say before he kissed me. I melted against him as he threaded his fingers through my hair.

His lips felt heavenly against mine, and I didn't resist when he pulled me into his lap, my back resting against the arm of the sofa. I lost track of time as we kissed. Shane pulled back and stared down at me, "I'm so glad you said yes."

I gave him a shy smile. This was new territory for me. I'd never made out this passionately with anyone before, nor had I sat in a guy's lap before. I had always been too afraid I'd hurt him. Shane seemed content with the way we were seated, though, so I didn't say anything.

Shane leaned in to kiss me again when I yawned. I was suddenly exhausted. I hadn't slept well all week, and now that I had finally relaxed my body, with the help of the wine, it was reminding me it needed rest.

"I'm sorry," I said, slightly embarrassed I had yawned in his face. "It's not you."

"I know, come on, let's go to bed."

Just because I had agreed to date him and had made out with him on my sofa didn't grant him automatic access to my bed. I gave him the same look I gave my patients when they did something outrageous. It had the desired effect because Shane held his hands up in surrender.

"I meant to sleep. Do you really think I'm going to let you alone all night so you can change your mind?"

I yawned again; at least this time, he wasn't trying to kiss me. Before I knew what was happening, Shane had scooped me up and was standing. I let out a panicked squeak. "What are you doing?"

"Carrying you to bed," he said with a grin. "No complaints, it's more for my benefit than yours."

I focused on not hyperventilating while we made the short trip to my bedroom. As soon as we were inside the door, I made him stop.

"We made it. You can put me down now."

"Sure thing," Shane said, switching his hold on me so that I slid down the front of his body before my feet touched the floor again. I was immediately turned on and impressed that he was moving me about like I weighed next to nothing. "So, do you want help changing or are we sleeping naked?"

My jaw dropped and I reached for the nearest thing available to throw at him. A stuffed bear my grandparents had given me for my seventh birthday, but before I could launch the bear at Shane, he had slipped out of my bedroom and closed the door with a soft click. He sure moved fast for such a large man.

"Just let me know when you're ready for me to come back in," he called through the door.

I walked to my closet and pondered what I should wear. I didn't have any fancy lingerie to impress him with, and I wasn't going to sleep in my underwear. *Calm down, he's already here; you don't have to impress him*, I rationalized to myself. I shed my clothes and pulled on a tank top and comfy cotton shorts before padding over to my bed. I crawled in and made sure I had the blankets covering myself before I called out to Shane.

"Ready when you are." I settled back against the pillows and waited for Shane to enter.

He was back in the room in seconds, closing the door behind him. I wasn't sure who he thought would walk in on us; I lived alone. I noticed that he had removed his shoes at some point as he walked over to my bed. A man hadn't been in my bedroom in over two years, and then only for a couple of hours; it was weird to think of Shane spending the night.

"Do you mind if I sleep in my boxers?" He asked, distracting me from my thoughts.

"No," I said, my mouth going dry. I was going to see Shane in his boxers. Calm down! You've seen him in swim trunks before; it's the same thing. *No, it's not*, the teenage girl inside me yelled, *he's never been in your bedroom in his swim trunks before, has he?* She had a point.

I watched as Shane made quick work of shedding his t-shirt and jeans. The man was beautifully made, all lean muscles and tan skin. It was hard not to drool. The bed sank slightly when he got in next to me.

"Relax, Lex, I won't bite." He paused, "At least not tonight." I shivered at the thought.

Shane pulled me over to him and then draped his arm over my hip, his hand resting on my stomach. Cuddling with Shane wasn't as weird as I thought it would be. I found myself relaxing into him as he played with my hair. I was almost asleep when I felt him kiss my neck and whisper, "Night, Lex."

"Night Shane, love you," I responded as I fell asleep.

Chapter 10

I woke up slowly. I needed to brush my teeth, and I had a slight wine headache. I lay there with my eyes closed, not relishing the idea of having to get out of bed, when I felt someone watching me. I slowly peeked through my lashes; Shane was sitting up in bed next to me watching me sleep. If he didn't look so cute, it would have been creepy.

"Why are you up already?" I asked, opening my eyes fully.

"Good morning, beautiful," he said. "Sleep well?"

"Mmhmm. You?" I asked, sitting up next to him.

"Not really, I was awake most of the night."

"I'm sorry. Any reason?"

"I was enjoying watching you sleep. Plus, I was thinking about what you said before you fell asleep." Shane was watching me intently, and I had to take a moment to figure out what I had said.

I had almost been asleep when Shane had kissed my neck and said good night and I had responded with... oh my god! I'd told Shane that I loved him. No wonder he had been up all night. I looked back at Shane, feeling myself start to turn red in embarrassment.

"Did you mean it," he asked, looking at me expectantly.

How did I answer that and not sound desperate or uninterested? Don't be a schmuck, just tell him the truth. What *was* the truth? How did I really feel about Shane? Who was I kidding? I had been in love with him for years; I just accepted that he would never feel the same.

"Yes," I said before I could come up with an excuse.

"I love you, too," Shane said, leaning in to kiss me.

"Wait! Wait! I need to brush my teeth," I said, grabbing the first excuse I could think of so I could take a minute to digest the fact that Shane had said he loved me too.

Shane laughed as I jumped out of bed and hurried into the en suite bathroom to scrub the fur off my teeth. When I returned, Shane was no longer in bed; in fact, he was no longer in my bedroom. I could feel the panic starting to bubble up when I saw his shirt lying on the floor at the foot of the bed. Where was he hiding?

I left the bedroom and found Shane wearing nothing but his jeans in my kitchen. My eyes were immediately drawn to his well-defined abs that disappeared below his waistband. Focus, you need to finish the conversation he started before you ran away.

"What are you doing?"

"I was going to make you breakfast, but it looks like you're running a little low on breakfast foods."

"I eat breakfast at work most days," I responded, stepping closer to him. "Do you really want to talk about breakfast right now?"

"What would you like to talk about?" He asked, giving me the bedroom eyes.

"This," I said as I wrapped my arms around his naked waist and tilted my face up to kiss him. Shane met me halfway, and I moaned lightly as our lips met. This was a thousand times better when I was awake and sober.

Shane ran his hands down my back to cup my ass and then pulled me closer. There was no space between us now, and I loved it. I bit his lower lip and was thrilled by his groan. Shane's hands slid lower onto my thighs, causing me to moan low in my throat.

One second I was standing, and the next I was seated on my kitchen counter with Shane standing in between my spread legs. This was accelerating faster than I had anticipated, but at the moment, I was more than okay with it. I ran my fingers through Shane's hair as he sucked on my bottom lip.

There was a knock on the kitchen door, and I groaned in disappointment. Shane bit down on my lip and slowly pulled away before letting it go. He took a step back and gave me a sexy grin.

"You should probably get the door," he said, giving me a wink.

"I'd rather continue what we were doing," I said, biting my bottom lip. "Whoever's at the door will come back later if it's important."

The person at the door knocked again, followed by Steph yelling, "I know you're in there." I groaned again and banged my head off the cabinet behind me.

Shane leaned in and kissed my forehead. "I love you."

"Come in," I yelled.

"Hi there, you two." Steph bounced in with a grin. "Am I interrupting something?"

"Not at all," I said, hopping down from the counter. "What brings you here, Steph?"

"Came to see if you two had made up yet. I've been waiting for years for you guys to figure out that you were in love." She paused when neither of us said anything, "Oh god, you didn't get to that part yet? Please tell me I didn't ruin this," she begged.

I shared a look with Shane before laughing. "You didn't ruin anything, Steph." I reassured her.

"I'm so happy for you guys," Steph said rushing over to gather us in a giant hug.

"Thanks Steph, I'm so happy you're okay with this." I told her, feeling tears forming.

"Now, I have something for you," she said, digging in her purse. "I wasn't sure if I would have to use these to make you two see reason or if you could use them after I left." She handed me the cuffs and Shane the key.

"Looks like I'll just be leaving these with you." Steph said with a wink as she closed the door behind her.

I couldn't help but laugh. Things were definitely looking up.

Don't miss out!

Visit the website below and you can sign up to receive emails whenever Liza Kline publishes a new book. There's no charge and no obligation.

https://books2read.com/r/B-A-MEXI-FSCBB

BOOKS2READ

Connecting independent readers to independent writers.

Did you love *Cuffed - A Novella*? Then you should read *The Trouble with Wedding Dates*[1] by Liza Kline!

MacKenzie's mom is hounding her to find a date for her sister's wedding but finding a suitable date is easier said than done when you have more curves than the average woman. As if that's not enough stress for one person to handle, throw in an unexpected visit from her best friend, Grant MacDaniels, at 2 AM that results in unexpected consequences.What's a girl to do when she's keeping secrets from everyone around her?

Read more at sweetanguish.com/lizakline/.

---

1. https://books2read.com/u/b5QVo7

2. https://books2read.com/u/b5QVo7

Also by Liza Kline

A Joyous Romance
Betrothed to the Vampire King
Married to the Vampire King
Mated to the Vampire King
A Joyous Romance Series Bundle (Books 1-3)

Standalone
Cuffed - A Novella
The Trouble with Wedding Dates
The Fall of Diablo
Fated
The Princess & the Monk

Watch for more at sweetanguish.com/lizakline/.

About the Author

Liza Kline lives in eastern Pennsylvania where she devours romance novels and chocolate while waiting for the zombie apocalypse. Until that day comes, Liza enjoys trips to the beach, designing websites, taking too many photos of sunsets and going to rock concerts.

Read more at sweetanguish.com/lizakline/.